In the middle of a forest lived three bears: a father bear, a mother bear, and a baby bear. They lived in a small thatched cottage. There was a pile of logs stacked by the door, along with a huge pair of black boots, a middle-sized pair of flowery boots, and a small pair of boots covered in raindrops.

One morning, Mother Bear was in the kitchen making breakfast. She put eight cups of oats and eight cups of milk into a saucepan. She stirred it with a wooden spoon, and soon the oatmeal was thick and bubbling.

First, Mother Bear spooned some oatmeal into a huge bowl. Then, she spooned some oatmeal into a middle-sized bowl, and then she scraped the oatmeal that was left into a small bowl.

The steam from the oatmeal curled up into the air. Father Bear came down the stairs and his huge black nose was twitching.
"Mmmm, I smell oatmeal!" he growled.

Baby Bear tumbled down the stairs next and rushed to the table. He put his paw out and touched the bowl of oatmeal.
"Ow!" he cried. "That's very, very hot!"

"Yes," said Mother Bear. "The oatmeal has just been cooked. As it's a lovely morning, let's go for a little walk and allow it to cool down."

So Father Bear, Mother Bear, and Baby Bear left the three bowls of oatmeal on the table, carefully shut the door to the cottage, and strolled off into the forest.

No sooner had the three bears vanished into the forest, than a girl with long, golden, curly hair ran out from the trees. Her name was Goldilocks. She flicked her long hair as she stopped and stared at the cottage.

“Perhaps whoever lives in this cottage can help me get back home,” said Goldilocks.
She knocked on the door and waited, but there was no reply.

Goldilocks tried the door. It opened, so she stepped into the cottage, calling, "Hello! Yoo-hoo!"
She looked around. The kitchen was very neat and tidy, and in the middle of it was a table with three bowls of steaming oatmeal on it. Goldilocks sniffed. The oatmeal smelled yummy.

Goldilocks suddenly felt very hungry. She hadn't had her breakfast yet, as she had gone out of the garden and into the forest before her mother and father had got up. Her mother and father always told her not to go into the forest by herself but she hadn't listened.

One of the chairs at the table was huge and heavy, but Goldilocks managed to force it back so that she could sit in it. Her feet didn't touch the ground. She knelt up on the huge chair, picked up the big spoon, and dipped it into the oatmeal.

"Yuck!" she cried. "This oatmeal is much too salty!"

Goldilocks got down and climbed onto the next chair. This chair was not quite as large but she still had to kneel on the seat to reach the oatmeal. She tasted it carefully.

"Yuck!" she spluttered. "This oatmeal is much too sweet!"

Goldilocks climbed onto the third chair, which was a good size for her. She tried the third bowl of oatmeal, which was not too salty and not too sweet. It was, in fact, just right. Goldilocks licked her lips and, before long, she had eaten it all up.

When she had finished, despite always being told not to by her mother, Goldilocks tipped the chair back and balanced it on its two back legs. The chair creaked and wobbled, and then broke. Goldilocks crashed to the floor.
"Ow!" she yelled.

Goldilocks went upstairs. In one bedroom there were two beds. One was a huge bed, which she only just managed to climb onto. She sank down into the bed, wrapping the quilt around her.
"Too soft!" she complained, as she struggled out of the huge bed.

The other bed in the room was not quite so large. Goldilocks climbed carefully onto this bed. Instead of sinking into it, she found she was lying on top of it, as if on a plank of wood.
"Too hard!" she huffed. "This is terrible. I cannot imagine anyone getting any sleep on this bed!"

In the other bedroom, Goldilocks found herself facing a lovely bed. It seemed to be just the right size for her. She snuggled into the quilt and pillows.
"This is lovely," she murmured, and in a very short space of time she had drifted off to sleep.

Meanwhile, the three bears returned from their walk and noticed that the door was now open. When they got inside, Mother Bear looked around and cried, “Oh no! Someone has tried a spoonful of my oatmeal!”

“...and mine,” growled Father Bear.

“Someone has eaten my oatmeal all up!” squeaked Baby Bear, “and they have smashed my chair into smithereens!”

As the three bears stood looking at the destroyed chair, they heard a noise from upstairs. It sounded like snoring. Father Bear climbed the stairs, with Mother Bear and Baby Bear sticking close behind him.

They stopped to look into Mother and Father Bear's bedroom.

"Someone has been in here," said Father Bear. "Look at the quilts. They are all crumpled up. That is not how we left them."

The snoring sound came again, and the three bears peered into Baby Bear's bedroom. Baby Bear started squeaking and jumping up and down.
"Look!" he said, pointing across the room. "Someone is sleeping in my bed!"

Father Bear roared and Goldilocks woke up with a start. The first thing she saw were the faces of the three bears. She screamed and hid under the quilt.
"Please don't hurt me!" she whimpered.

“Hurt YOU?” roared Father Bear. “You are the one who has entered our house, eaten our oatmeal, smashed Baby Bear’s chair, and slept in our beds!”

Goldilocks peeked out from under the quilt.
“I’m sorry,” she said in a small voice. “I did knock but no one replied. The oatmeal smelt so lovely, but I didn’t mean to eat it all... and I didn’t mean to smash the chair or fall asleep.”

Goldilocks helped Baby Bear sweep up the bits of broken chair, while Mother Bear made more oatmeal. Then the three bears took Goldilocks home.
"Thank you so much," she said. "I am very sorry about barging into your house without being invited. I hope we can be friends now."

Baby bear gave Goldilocks a hug.
"Come and visit us next week and share our oatmeal," he said. "This time you are invited!"